SOMETHIN

Josie Blaine

Something About Sophia
by Josie Blaine

FIRST EDITION
ISBN: 978-0-9895554-1-8

Published by Happy Publishing

Printed in the United States of America

Acknowledgements and Appreciation

In 2009, my dear friend and fellow writer Tammy Lunkenheimer and I were drinking coffee in her kitchen.

"You should write a novel," she suggested, out of the blue.

Now, let me tell you that I've written short stories, news, commercials for TV and radio, in my diary and on grocery lists, but had not considered putting any of my work into a bound form. Thank you, Tammy.

The idea of a book would not go away. The subject for the novel came to me one hot afternoon in Gruene Coffee Haus in New Braunfels, while chatting with a traveling genealogist. This led me to hours upon hours of conversation with Grandma in North Dakota, who had been sharing family legends with me since I was old enough to listen. I would need to write them down. Moreover, I would have to move to North Dakota to do so.

I asked Grandma about Sophia, and she told me not much was known about this woman who had braved the Dakota Territory so long ago, when the land was wild. Her story was very vague, while the history of my great-great grandfather was meticulously recorded.

My appreciation extends to the North Dakota

Historical Society, Heritage Center and Archives, where I spent countless hours, delving into my family history and reading about my great-great grandfather. I recommend we learn about our personal histories while we have parents and grandparents to teach us.

The New Salem Historical Society continues to preserve the Christiansen House, and for that, I am thankful. I have been fortunate to spend time in the home library of my great-great grandparents, and see what they enjoyed, and the awards my grandfather won for his work in agriculture and ranching education in the early days of this state.

Thank you, Pamela Brinkworth Rutyna and Emily Risty, my editors. My dear friends and family, who have endured bicentennial discussions with me for the last four years, I thank you. I pondered this story for a long time. When I met Publisher Erica Glessing, I began to consider finishing it. The day my mother read six pages and told me she loved it, I became not only a writer, but an author. Thank you, Mom.

Sincerely,
Josie

"Let us not forget the contributions ... of the pioneer woman."

— John Christiansen

Pioneering western America depended on the droves pouring through Ellis Island in the Nineteenth Century. Railcars loaded with dreams of the New World wound through the plains, carrying Manifest Destiny to where new farms, cities and homes would be built. Dogs, families, and pianos ringing out from churches of the future depended on the railroad tracks of yesteryear.

Many new Americans settled in Iowa, Wisconsin, and Illinois, for that was as far west as most people had ever gone. Adventurers and fur traders had travelled beyond the Mississippi, further west, and had brought back bigger furs, more exotic stories, and some had not come back at all. The west, it seemed, was truly wild.

Not only was it wild, but largely uninhabited. The railroad folks knew they could profit from a more populated route. This is but one story of when the western run was won.

Franceska

CHRISTIAN PRESSED ON, WITH EVERY BIT OF strength he had. He felt the muscles in his back tense and release with every push, as he moved his plow and tilled the sod. He stopped to look up, and across the field, at Franceska, his beloved, sitting on the stool outside their small house, her hands plunging into the basin and folding the clean bedclothes. In the breeze, her long golden mane glistened in the burgeoning sunset. She looked up, saw him looking her way, and waved. Her wide smile gave him the strength to plow another ten acres. He would plow two hundred, for Franceska. Even at the other end of the earth.

As the afternoon sun began to lazily fall on the western Bavarian hills, the young farmer straightened up and wiped his brow. He smiled to himself as he lumbered toward the cottage, where fresh laundered shirts and sheets waved in the soft breeze. The wheat was coming up nicely now. It would be a good fall. Today was a good day. It was a good life.

Theirs was a one-room cottage, mortared together by his great grandfather a hundred years ago. Its walls were not tall, but tall enough for a man to stand proudly in his home. It was not large, but it was large enough to hold the great love of a family. Christian knew that a man had to build his own house, work his own land, and create his own world, in order to be a man. His father would send a hired servant at harvest to inspect the crop. Christian would not disappoint him.

Christian stopped to pull an ear of corn off of its stalk, and grab two carrots out of the rich, life-giving earth. He brushed the dirt off of them, and held each piece of produce up to the western sun to admire its perfection, and proceeded in the direction of the house to present these gifts to his wife.

Christian had taken Franceska as his bride last winter. It was a marriage arranged by their parents, who were neighboring farmers. Christian's father gave him a strip of land, and Franceska's father gave him an equal strip of land, meaning Christian's farm, between his father's farm and that of his father-in-law, was fairly sizable. It looked healthy, and they were happy. Their families were nearby, but newlyweds need their own place, their own space, to learn how to depend on each other. One day, he would preside over all three farms. He had no brothers. Franceska's sister had gone off to the nunnery. Reflecting on this, Christian reached down to sift the soil betwixt his fingers. He was attached to this ground.

As he neared the cottage, his nose picked up the smell of Franceska's stew. He marched through the door of their home, and announced to her that he was finished for the day, and hungry. He proudly presented the corn and carrots, and his wife promptly added them to the venison stew. Ah, yes, Christian smiled to himself, his wife was cooking the deer he had killed and hung on the tree earlier in the week. Christian was impressed to see Franceska had baked bread into golden bowls. He would have asked her how she had done that, but it was woman's work, and she did not ask him about the fields. When the carrots were tender, Franceska ladled a portion of the hearty stew she'd been simmering all day into each bread bowl, and served her husband supper at the little wooden table in the middle of their stone kitchen.

When they had finished eating, and the dogs lay, happily gnawing on the meat bones, the two young lovers gazed into each other's eyes, by the firelight from the hearth, Christian thought Franceska looked especially tired tonight. Within months, he would learn why she seemed weary.

They were blessed with their first child, a son, at Easter. Christian named him John. Christian's father and mother brought gifts. Franceska's family prepared a vast spread of food and a group of musicians, crowded onto a wagon, played all day long, into the night. It was a feast, prepared in celebration of the son.

Something About Sophia

NORTH DAKOTA, 1984

THE DELICATE WHITE FABRIC OF MY FAVORITE dress matched the season. It was springtime in North Dakota, and my mom had bought me lavender knee socks and jelly shoes to match the roses on this dress, for my piano recital. I had an oversized lavender bow in my permed, bobbed hair. After all, this was The Nineteen Eighties, and I was about to show the parents and other students that I was totally awesome.

Every jelly step clicked from the floor of the First Lutheran Church basement up through my ten-year-old legs, along my spine, tingled along my arms, and made my hands tremble as I approached the piano. My parents, along with everyone else's parents, were seated in the folding chairs marked FIRST LUTHERAN CHURCH, waiting to hear me knock out my renditions of, "Flashdance: What a Feeling," and bring down the house with, "Edelweiss."

I had practiced that song until I could play it in my sleep, on my piano at home in our living room on Sixth Street. My practice time interrupted after-school TV time, much to my big brother's shouting chagrin and painful pestering, but it made me so happy, and feel so grown up to be able to bring beautiful sound out of that beautiful, big heirloom, which to me, was as big as the wall in our huge old house. When my dad came home from work, he would sit in his recliner, eyes closed, completely oblivious to any mistake I'd make, just pleased as he could be to listen to me play piano while Mom finished making dinner. I think he was happy to relax after work, and that he was seeing some return on his investment in my musical education. My piano teacher was a dear friend of my parents, a gymnastics instructor, and a member of the local ambulance squad. In a small town, one person must fulfill several roles, to keep the town going. Cyndie, my piano teacher, was adamant that I practice, every spare moment.

The piano in our house had been in the family for generations. From the time I was very small, my grandma would recount the legend over and over, that this had been my great-great grandmother's piano, and had survived The Great Chicago Fire. More than one hundred years earlier, Chicago was a young and bustling city.

CHICAGO, 1870

PEOPLE WERE BUILDING. THOUSANDS OF NEW Americans from every direction were building their businesses, houses and apartment buildings along the shore of Lake Michigan. The Midwestern trees provided plenty of lumber for the cause of housing, and the surrounding forests were razed and became farmland.

We were also new Americans. Father was a sailor man. He'd sailed with the German Imperial Navy, in his younger days, and he was quite the adventurer. He was jovial with a serious jaw. He had tales to tell about every port and storm swell. He had sailed the Seven Seas, he would say, and when he heard of a popular migration to the New World, he thought he must go. The political seas in Europe were tossing and turning in those days, and like a sailor would, my father looked beyond the horizon.

Armies were being raised in such a way they never had before, and people were more tightly restricted from moving around the countryside. The government was putting pressure on farmers. My father saved up his money for his new home in the New World, and when he left Germany, he was able to keep his money and bought his passage aboard the immigrant ship by working as a sailor. It was an icy, fourteen-day voyage across the Northern Atlantic Ocean. Father would tell stories of how frightened all the passengers were, aboard the ship, how they would collectively scream and moan, when the ship would pitch and toss. For these people, it was their first voyage. My father had sea legs. He was at home on the waves, and would joke that he could "walk on water."

The emigrants wondered what on earth they had gotten themselves into. They had left everything they had, which was not much, so that they could die on these rough seas with their children?

Whole families had uprooted themselves and climbed aboard ships, armed with their faith and dreams and what little possessions remained after buying their way onto the boat. The two-week sail across the ocean was not easy on them. The waters were so rough and the waves were so high, tossing the ship every which way, no one knew if they were still on course to make it to New York. The captain watched the stars, and all passengers — every man, woman and child — had to help bail the water out of the boat with buckets, and boots, or with any vessel they could find. So many of them were sick, and weary of sea travel. He tried to stay away from the sick ones, because if you were sick when you got to New York, they would send you back to Germany. No one was sick in America. America was a land of healthy, robust bodies, and souls who could dream and were well enough, and strong enough to work those dreams into reality. America was where my father wanted to be, more than anything.

In the early hours of the fourteenth morning, Father was swabbing the deck of the Frieda Lorenz after two weeks of sailing. Rain continued to fall and aid him in his task, and though it stung his face, he was thankful. His duty was to wash the sickness from the boards of the deck.

During this somewhat unpleasant task, Father tells of the moment he fell in love with his new country.

"Through the rain and high waves, I saw her," he would tell the story again and again. He could almost feel the warmth of liberty shining on his face, as if this very new country was welcoming him, her harbour gesturing like a loving mother with open arms, whose prodigal son had been away too long. He began to thank God then, and there, through the hot tears of joy, which were mixed with cold raindrops falling down his face.

He promised he would do his best for America. He would be the man America needed him to be.

After landing on Ellis Island, in New York, my father stood in long, slow lines with all the others from the ship. They were all full of hope for what they would be able to do for their families without the oppression they faced in the countries from whence they came. They embraced the United States. Many of them knew a few words of English, and were able to communicate across the culture lines with those words: "Hungry. Tired. Work. Family."

They waited with trepidation for a long time in the lines, which took what seemed like days. They had no choice but to submit to humiliating medical exams and education tests, during which examiners would decide if the new immigrants were healthy or intelligent enough to move forward. Finally, the people in the lines were directed to a line that would decide their destiny. Here, the stairs forked into three directions: one stairway would lead them into New York City, which was not necessarily a bad direction at all. Another stairway led travelers to a ship that took them back to Europe if they did not pass the exams, because the sick or illiterate were not to be allowed in America. Everyone knew that. America was too pure, too untouched, to allow the sick. People had helped each other on the immigrant ship. They studied Bible verses, so that they would be able to show that they could read upon landing at Ellis Island. The final stairway, and the most fortuitous, would lead immigrants to a train which would be going westward, to the great beyond of America, the land of opportunity and blessings, the reason they had come all this way.

One small girl had a mark on her coat, where examiners had drawn an "X" with chalk, due to a watery red eye and runny nose. Her mother was overcome with silent weeping, clinging to the family's Holy Bible, and her father looked stern and worried. Father said they would have had to send the little girl back to Europe or put her in the hospital, and they had no money, and the rest of the family was here in New York now, standing on this island. What were they to do?

"We've done everything right," the little girl's father said. "She isn't ill. We've done everything right. We can read. English."

Thinking quickly, and before many people noticed her mark, my father reached down, slipped the girl's coat from her shoulders and turned it inside out, then helped her put it back on. This way, her family could move westward, unmarked, with their hope intact.

My father was thrilled and relieved to be going west, because many of the other Germans were going that way. That train meant a future, possibly a farm one day, and it meant that he could begin dreaming. He had not allowed himself to think past today for a long time. He thought he would be most comfortable staying with the other Germans. On that train, he saw a pretty girl, with eyes like the sea, so he jostled his meager possessions and traded seats with different passengers on the train until he was able to sit next to her.

Her name was Amelia. She was traveling alone, because her mother and father had sent her away when her older brothers had been drafted into the Russian army and had been taken away from the family. They had received word from others, who had already emigrated, that German girls could find employment in the America, and German was spoken nearly everywhere. Amelia's parents believed their daughter would be safer in America than if she would have stayed in Germany during these unsettling times. They saw their farm shrinking, as more and more land was taken away by Catherine the Great and her Russian army. With Stephen and Edward gone, there would be no one to work the fields that were left. They did not want to set Amelia on a track to such a hard life. They kissed their daughter and put her on a ship, with all the fortune they could spare, including a few family heirlooms for safekeeping in the New World.

Since they were both alone in this new country, my father and this pretty girl chatted and talked the entire way to Ohio, when many of the people got off of the train. They looked at each other, in the eyes, and agreed that since each was the only person they knew in America, they would go further west, to Chicago, together. He had heard of the prosperity to be had on the docks of the Great Lakes, which were practically another ocean, and she could most likely find work as a housekeeper or a secretary. She planned on making a nice life for herself, so she could send good news back to her mother and her father in Germany.

Upon arriving in Illinois, he landed a job working on the ships. They needed good men in every industry in this city, and as my father always said about Germans, "God forbid we should not work." I don't know exactly where the ships went, but he was gone for long stretches of time. He was hungry for heroism, and where there was hard work, danger, excitement, adventure, or uncharted waters, heroism was hungry for my father.

John and Amelia were married very soon after reaching Chicago. They settled into the German community, and were wed in a simple ceremony. The ladies of the church gathered flowers and prepared a feast. Amelia felt honored and very special, though she was sorry her mother and father were not in attendance.

My brother, Gustav, was born when I was four. He was precious to us, and he had my mother's eyes. He wanted to engineer trains when he grew. I pretended he was my own toy doll, and I could cuddle him, swaddle him and play with him. He was my forever friend, my sweet brother. We played quietly inside, and we ran in the safety of our neighborhood with the other children nearby. We feared nothing, because there was nothing to fear. Everyone was our family.

When I was a young child and my brother was still very small, Chicago burned. The houses and buildings in those days were all built of wood, of course, and when one caught fire, many would follow. My father was a strong man, and a quick thinker. He had good humor about him, and people listened to him. He could make people act, and he could make people laugh. In the fire, he rescued many Chicagoans and their families. Because of his leadership, the men of our neighborhood saved many homes from certain ruin, and many children from burning. Many homes are still standing because my father, the seaman, knows how to use water, and make water fly. Trajectory, he called it. I was just a very little girl, but I remember that our German neighborhood would have been decimated by the fire if not for my father and the way people listen to him, the authority in his words, and the lives he changes just by being around them. My father will go down in history.

My mother — oh, my mother was beautiful. She had the most sparkling, blue-green eyes. Her eyes were the color of the sea when the sun dances on the water, and I can imagine that is most likely why my father fell in love with her. Looking into her eyes was like looking at the ocean, and he always was at home on the ocean. Looking into her eyes was like being home.

She loved music, and we would play the piano and sing old German songs and new American songs. Whenever his ship would come in, my mother wound up her phonograph in the parlor, and she and father would dance downstairs in the parlor all night long.

One day as I walked home from school, after the fire, the neighborhood had a different feeling about it. I held my strap of books tighter to my side. There was an anxiety on our street that I had not felt before, and I saw all of the neighbors frantically seeking whatever it was they were looking for. I entered our house to find Mother hysterical. Gustav was nowhere to be found, and she had been running from door to door, and our friends and neighbors, and people from the church, were now fanning out to inspect every Gustav-sized space in the city, because he had to be found. He had to be brought home. It would be dark in a few hours, and Gustav was absolutely afraid of the dark. We would not leave him alone out there in the dark.

Torches and gaslights burned all night. Mother did not sleep at all. Gustav was gone, into air, into stillness, and it brought on our house a sadness so deep and dark that after not long, pain could no longer hurt. Father was away at that time, on his ship, and we did not know when he was coming home to learn this horrible nightmare. In the newspapers, we would read of other families that had lost a child and would sometimes take another to replace that child, to continue the family line. It was common, if the child was small enough, with no questions and no answers. But why, oh why, did our Gustav go? His trains were everywhere in the house and yard, and there was not a moment of any day when I did not wonder where my brother was. I knew it would be the same for my mother and my father.

My mother was my best friend, my closest confidante, for she understood my life, my quietness, my secrets, and we shared the pain of losing Gustav. Father was away on the ship much of the time, and my mother was with me. Like most German women, she took a hard pride in the handling of her household. We swept the front step every morning, to sweep away any bad luck or dark spirits, and not a speck of dust remained anywhere in the house when we lay down at night.

I was nine when Gustav disappeared, and oh, how we searched for him. The neighborhood sought my small brother for weeks, and we could not find him. Father was sailing. He never quite gets that pain out of his eyes. He had the pained look that his boy is gone, his only son. I knew, without it being said, he knew some other family was raising his son or someone had hurt him in some way that could never be mentioned or understood. Father has the wise eyes of a sailor, a hero, a man who has seen terrible things. Not knowing the whereabouts of his son weighs on him and has torn a part of his soul, as if his hull was broken.

I hoped someone would be there to hold Gustav if he fell, to bandage his skinned knees, to kiss his hurts. We never spoke of him again, for it could be bad luck to Gustav, if we keep his name on our lips. He is always in our hearts, and we will never stop loving him. He never ages for me. I still see the child, with his trains, asking me to play with him. Anytime I hear the long, lonesome whistle of a train, I know Gustav is on it, somewhere.

HARVESTER

There was a murmur in the streets, and it rose to a clamor. Mother's oceanic eyes began to spark, and well up. Father was due home in a day, and a schooner reported a burning ship out in the sea. I knew it would not be his. His crew of twenty-five had carried iron, grain, and lumber countless times. I knew my father's crew was helping this burning ship. He is a hero, my father. When danger presents itself, he rides high the wave and makes everything right again. When there is danger, people stay close to my father, because they know they will be alright.

Night fell, and in the dark outside our warm house, it was too dangerous to go looking for news. Our neighborhood that was pleasant and clean and safe during the daylight hours, was not so safe at night, for lately there had been people being robbed. Hoodlums would take them for all they had, money, food, even a man's coat, if they were out walking at night. When we lost Gustav, we lost the innocence of the neighborhood. Other families began to worry that their children would disappear, and so I was instructed to stay very close to my mother.

Mother and I busied ourselves with the last of tomorrow morning's chores, so that if tomorrow he should return, it could be spent welcoming Father home and hearing his spirited seafaring tales. We cleaned, and even baked his favorite kuchen, with peaches that Mother had purchased from the market in the train yard. Farmers brought their produce from the southern lands to market to people in the north. A kind farmer from Georgia brought peaches that my mother liked. We had seen him before on our trips to the market.

He told us that people were poor in the South, but the fields were rich. He was traveling to sell fruit to support his family. Mother told me that if Father had gone to a seaside dock somewhere, to sell the fruit of his fields, she prayed families would give him a fair price for the work of his hands.

We baked many loaves of bread, in case he brought home with him survivors of that burning ship. They would be hungry, Mother noted.

The house was warm, and smelled of fresh kuchen. Mother folded the blanket and laid it over the back of her rocking chair, and told me no more could be done tonight, and tucked me into my bed, deep under three quilts she'd stitched and embroidered with lace and flowers. My face sank into the cool pillow that had been airing in the breeze on the open windowsill all day.

I drifted to dreamland, and there we were — Mother, Father, Gustav and I, together riding on a train. Father had been telling us for a long time that one day he would take us on a train ride. I don't know where we were going, but it didn't matter. Father said Gustav could be in charge, he could engineer the train. We laughed and sang joyful travel songs, and Mother had packed a picnic, and oh, it tasted so good. We ate jelly sandwiches and cheese and drank coffee while Gustav drove the train. Mother made cake for this trip! The sun shone so brightly on the countryside. The hills may well have been carpeted with gold, so brightly did the wheat shimmer in the sunshine. I didn't need to know where we were going, because my father knew, and the railroad tracks knew. There was no way to go wrong.

A crash and a cry woke me. It sounded like the door broke in, and I half-fell, half-leaped out of my bed, and peered around the doorjamb. With my small lantern, I tiptoed to my mother's room, looking for her, but she was not there. I was afraid, and my heart began to pound. I wanted to hide under her bed, where I would be safe until daylight, but I was enticed by the noises downstairs. My mind began to race — perhaps father was home early, perhaps he just burst into the parlor and they were celebrating his homecoming with friends, perhaps there are burglars down there. Holding onto the banister, I leaned over as far as I could to see down the stairs.

There, on the parlor floor, lying in front of the hearth, was my mother, and there was blood from her head, so much more blood than I had ever seen before. She wasn't moving. I froze. Mrs. Knirk, our neighbor, was frantically praying out loud. Mr. Rusch, from our church, picked up the heavy door and leaned it against its hinges again. I cried out, and they saw me. Friends and other neighbors began to gather in the doorway, and two men immediately went to work fixing the door. I ran to Mrs. Knirk and threw my arms around her.

"There's kuchen," I heard my own raspy voice whisper, trying to be the good hostess my mother had raised me to be. If Mrs. Knirk had come to the house on any afternoon, she would be served whatever freshly baked goods were in our kitchen. The same held true for any of our neighbors, and the men fixing the door. My mind was racing and I was thinking about every single thing that was happening. I must be giving. I must be gracious. Be sweet.

She held me tightly and hid my eyes, and stroked my hair. She told me not to be afraid. The only world I had in that moment was fear. My father was not here. My mother was not awake. Gustav was somewhere else, and I missed him more in that moment than I ever had in my life. Even though he was my younger brother, to have a sibling at a moment like this would have been much more comforting. I wouldn't be alone, even with all of these people around. Mother always knew the right thing to do at the right moment, and my mind did not comprehend why she could not get up. Why is she asleep, and why is there so much blood?

As the minutes and hours passed, and Mother continued to lie motionless on the parlor floor, the details became clearer. She had gone to the pier, after I'd gone to sleep. She'd run to the lighthouse in the dark, to see if she could see his ship, to watch for him coming home to us, for this had been a longer-than-usual trip. It was that time of year in Chicago when the streets and rocks and steps get slick, and my mother fell. She fell from I don't know where, the steps or the widow's walk at the top of the lighthouse, or the rocky climb, but she fell. Mr. Rusch, doing a voluntary Citizen's Patrol of the pier at the right time, saw her fall and ran to her. Of course he recognized her, despite the gash on her forehead and the blood pouring forth. Mr. Rusch carried her all the way back to our house, crying out for help along the way. Mrs. Knirk heard him in the street, from inside her own house, and ran outside to help bring her home.

They brought her home, and Mrs. Knirk had sent Mr. Knirk to gather the doctor after he knocked down our door. Dr. Patrick appeared just then, as if out of a mist. The crowd let him through, and he set his black bag on the floor as he knelt beside Mother's head.

I heard him say words I had never heard before as he examined her, because they sounded unpleasant, and these were not part of our vernacular. Contusion, lobe, paralyzed, broken.

Dr. Patrick bandaged her head tightly, and advised that we would know nothing more until daybreak, or later. We had to try to get Mother to awaken, in order for anything to happen. We could not stand in the parlor and watch her forever. But tomorrow, my father was coming home, and now, there is blood on the floor. My mother would have thrown a holy German fit if she knew the neighbors were in her parlor and there was anything out of place. She always kept the house as neat as a pin.

I ran to the pantry to get the soap and bucket. I sought out the rags Mother and I had used just yesterday in our cleaning. I would clean up this mess, for when she woke up, she wouldn't want to see blood. She'd be angry, upset, or feel sad and guilty. I don't like when she's anything but calm. The world is unsettled if my mother is not happy. I focused hard on the sounds. The tin bucket, banging against the doorjamb and the furniture because I was so nervous, I was shaking. The rags made a squishing sound when I squeezed them and wrung them out in the bucket, then scrubbed on the floor, next to my mother, who lay so very still. I did not know then, if tomorrow would ever come. I almost hoped it wouldn't.

The sun hinted of its awakening over our German neighborhood, as my mother's bleeding slowed, with the tightness of the doctor's bandages, and Dr. Patrick announced that her breathing was calmer. She was so pale, and so cold. As the forenoon wore on, I extinguished the candles and turned down the fire, I closed the fireplace doors, so heat would escape but the smoke would leave through the chimney. I did not want Mother breathing in smoke.

The doctor and Mr. Rusch carried her to her big, comfortable bed, and Mrs. Knirk helped me tuck her in. We made sure her head was elevated, so she would not get the cough. Mr. Rusch went home. At my urging, because I knew Mother would have insisted, he ate a good portion of the peach kuchen on his way out of the house. Mrs. Knirk promised to come back later in the day and check on us, and she went home, too. It being the wee hours of the morning, I brought one of the quilts from my bed and curled up on the chair next to my mother's bed, and gazed at her, sleeping peacefully and motionless.

I cannot even imagine the thoughts that go through one's mind as they ascend a lighthouse like Grosse Pointe, focusing Heavenward, unexpectedly slip on some ice and begin to fall one hundred and nineteen feet to an uncertain fate below. Did she immediately lose consciousness? Did her life flash before her eyes? Was she thinking about me? Was she thinking about Gustav? Father? There she'd been, gazing seaward, into the black, black night, longing for his ship to come in, perhaps her last thought was a prayer for him to catch her.

I must have slept well into that afternoon, because birds were singing and the afternoon sun was already fading to the west windows when my eyes blinked open. Mother had not moved. In the distance, I could hear a train. I wondered where Gustav was at this moment. Oh, I wish I had a brother today. I was terrified, and Father wasn't here, and Mother was, in every way that mattered at this moment, not here. I needed my brother. He'd been gone from my life, our lives, for ten years now, and he would be fourteen. If he were with us, with me, we would have so much fun. I would teach him all the things he needed to know about succeeding at the Evangelical School. I would make his favorite kuchen, just for him, and maybe a strudel to celebrate special occasions. We would run down to the train tracks every time we'd hear the locomotive approach, and pump our arms into the air, begging the engineer to blow the horn. If he did bend to our wishes and blow the horn, we would feel as though we'd altered time and space, and maybe we had a little bit of control over the universe, if only for that brief moment in time. If my little brother were here today, I would teach him these things. It was hard to be an only child, scary to be alone, when Mother is so ill, and Father is away on a voyage, no telling when he would be home. I needed my brother to be here with me.

The heavy front door burst open, and that booming, comforting voice I loved so dearly rang through the hall. I ran to meet him, and leaped into his arms, allowing every tear that I had been holding back today to pour out of me. I prepared him for the sight he was about to see, and I led him by the hand to Mother. I told him about the news of a burning ship, and how she'd gone to look for him after tucking me in to sleep. And she'd fallen. He kneeled at her side and wept.

The reaction of my big, strong, heroic father surprised me, and yet, did not. I stood there a long time, watching my parents. This was my new reality, my new world. I wasn't sure where it would go from here, but I was certain yesterday was no more. Just then, some miracle began to flicker in my house. Mother's eyelids opened. She looked, first up at me, then at my father, and closed her eyes again and smiled. He not only wept, but cried now, in deafening silence. There were no more tears, but sobs that knocked the wind out of his lungs. It shook me to see my father showing this much emotion. It began to register in my mind that what we were dealing with was something more than just sleep. My father was a hero, through the entire scene. He was so strong, impenetrable. And my mother was sleeping. I did not understand.

She opened her eyes a few more times in the following days. She never said anything, she just opened her eyes, and looked as if on watch, as if on the widow's walk, waiting for her true love's ship to appear on the horizon, for him to come home to her. Then, she would close her eyes again. Dr. Patrick recommended placing her in an asylum, for there was nothing more to be done for her. Father angrily scoffed at such an idea, for as long as she needed us, we would take care of her, he said. We were her family. No one else would touch her.

We'd heard of people who were put away in asylums. They would lie in their beds and rot away, because the nurses would not feed the ones that did not talk. There was no way my beautiful mother would go into a place like that. Not while my father and I both breathe.

The day Mother awoke was joyous for us — me, Father, the entire neighborhood. Mrs. Knirk had been helping us move her arms and legs, because she told me Mother didn't want to be stiff when she wakes. So she slept for three days and finally awoke.

Neighbors, friends, and people from church came by to wish us well, and to bring food. We had more food than the three of us would ever eat, but that is how it is done in this close community.

It wasn't perfect. She could not speak, but could only moan quietly, so quietly it really was more of a whisper or a murmur. She could not walk, or move her arms. I thought this was my fault, if she was stiff, because I did not stretch her arms and legs enough while she was sleeping.

He stayed home to take care of Mother while I was in school, and when his ship would sail, I would stay home with her. We took care of her for four years, with no change in her condition. She would get terrible respiratory disease, and so many times I thought we were going to lose her.

In my eighteenth winter, Chicago was particularly blustery. The wind was relentless, and Father had gone on a short sail. We ran out of firewood, and I was sleeping in Mother's bed to keep her warm. In the morning I woke, and she was cold. She was so terribly cold, no matter how many quilts I tucked around her, I could not make her warm. I snuggled up against her, and talked to her a little about what the day might bring. I would make her a porridge, Mrs. Knirk would come over for tea, and we would sing her some of the old songs. She did not react to my words like she normally did.

My mother died in her sleep on a November night, before Thanksgiving, and after All Saints' Day. She loved holidays, and family gatherings, and baking Christmas breads for people she barely knew. She loved every soul she met, was the mother of two, and the wife of one.

Father went back on the ship. I went back to the Evangelical School for Girls. My friends knew about my mother, and no one knew what to say, I suppose, which is why no one said a word. And these three remain: Faith, Hope, and the Charity that is Love. I believed it was my mission to give myself to other people, to help other people. A good German would help anywhere she could.

I didn't cry. I did whimper twice: once when I tried making the chokecherry jelly by myself for the first time, and Mrs. Knirk rescued me when I got stuck and did not know how much sugar to add to the fruit. Again, I became emotional when I was embroidering a quilt block for the quilt I'd started with my mother's pattern, and the lace came together so lovely, that I thought for sure her hand had been in it. Oh, I wanted to show it to her, it turned out so pretty. I did not cry. I felt that would have been disrespectful to my mother's strong memory. Germans don't, you see. We see things through. Strength is honor. I would honor her by not shedding tears. I was a woman, not a child. I would face the future with a strong jaw, and make my mother proud and be level for my father. He would not see me weaken.

To watch Father without Mother broke my heart daily. Caring for her was like breathing, it had become our lives. When she died, there was an emptiness, a space that could not be filled by anything else — any food, activity, or music, for Chicago still was my mother.

Chicago still ached of her, and the air filling every space around my body pierced my skin with the pain of losing someone I loved so much. She was my mother. I am of her flesh. Everything I am, is because of her. She taught me to walk, talk, sing, dance, laugh, be joyous, and worship. She taught me the old ways, the German ways.

That winter, there was a buzzing in the churches around the German neighborhoods. The railroads were sending colonists out west and starting new cities for them. In the past, the west had been known for savages and buffalo, but now the government said the colonists would get their own land, and they could farm on it or raise cattle or build businesses and houses. When the opportunity arose to go to Dakota Territory, Father said we were going, and that was that. He'd come from Germany, not to stay in a city, but to breathe the fresh air of his own homestead. He wanted to explore and see just how much room there was out there. People said the land went on forever, and the government was giving it away! Back in Germany, Father said, they had to beg and plead and scratch for a scrap of dirt to grow food, because things were getting so bad. He said we never heard from the relatives there anymore, and he never expected to hear from them again. It could mean they had died, and we should pray for their souls, he said. It was time to move on.

Kuchen Bars

1 c. butter
1 c. sugar
2 eggs
1 tsp. vanilla
2 c. flour
fruit
Top layer:
1 ¾ c. cream
4 eggs
½ c. sugar
1 heaping T. tapioca
cinnamon and sugar

Beat butter, sugar, eggs, vanilla and flour. Pat into jelly roll pan.

Layer on well-drained fruit or fresh fruit.

Beat well the cream, eggs, sugar and tapioca. Pour over fruit. Sprinkle with cinnamon and sugar.

Bake at 350° for 45 to 50 minutes.

Away From the Sunrise

I AM NOT SURE HOW BIG THE SKY IS THAT HOSTS the stars on the edge of Chicago, but it is colossal. It never ends. Stargazing, my father would say, is for youth and sailors.

He said this was for me, that we could not stay here in the great sadness anymore. It was time to go. This, this is why he'd left Germany for The New World — America. He came to make a better way for me before he ever knew me, and we would go to Dakota Territory so my children, someday, would have that entire sky. We signed up for the charter, and began to whittle down our belongings to what we would need. Father said we would close up the house and leave it. Someone would take it for themselves, or Mr. Rusch would keep an eye on it for us. It was time to take Germany with us, to spread our love for Deutschland to the next-western part of this great land. Who knew how vast America is? It may go on forever.

Father closed the front door of the house on Walnut Street and we climbed into the carriage that would take us to the train depot. I shivered in the Lake Michigan breeze, which had a bone-chilling grip on winter that refused to give way to spring. Our house, with our furniture inside, hiding under dust cloths, waved goodbye to us from the curtains still hanging in the upstairs windows. Father said he was not concerned with the furniture or the house. We had sold what we could. The rest was in the care of the church. Now, we were in the care of the church. Truly, we were stepping out on faith, that this was the right path. We were leaving behind the sad emptiness that was the loss of my brother and my mother.

We would embark on a new adventure…If it weren't for the ricketiness of this train, it would feel like a baby carriage, and I would sleep the entire way to Dakota Territory. I am going with Father on an adventure, to be part of an Evangelical Synod colony, and to own our own farm, and grow our own food. We would depend on no one else. In fact, Father told me that because I am now eighteen, I can stake my own claim. I can own my own land. I had never considered that before, but now I could start allowing my mind to make plans.

The New Garden of Eden

DAKOTA TERRITORY, 1882

I ENVISIONED MY FUTURE — IT WOULD BE BEAUTIFUL.
The farmstead is laid out in a very orderly fashion,
like a good German would do it, and the sun shining on the grass makes it look like silk in the after
noon breeze. There are children — my children? — playing in the farmyard, and they are blonde, with bright
blue eyes and mischievous smiles. They've been into the
silo again, though I have scolded them time and again,
no, and stop that. The lush tree line surrounding our
place protects us from the really harsh winter, so the
children can play outside all year round, which is impor
tant to me when I need to do my ironing and sewing.

I have a porch and a flower garden that is the envy
of the town. There is a white picket fence and a stone
path leading to the street, and it is just perfect. Fireflies
light in our trees, and Father lives next door, and there

is a hammock between our two places.

The train stopped and I awoke with a start. Father, a rather stoic man, chuckled at my alarm.

We gathered what things we had, and stepped off the train. It was April, and there was no smell of slaughterhouse in the air. It was so clean, the air, I felt like the breeze was blowing right through me, everything that had hurt me over the last few years was blowing away. Now that I was a resident of the Dakota Territory, I was going to let it blow away everything inside me, until the pain was gone. I was going to let that wind give me a fresh, clean start. I would still miss my mother, I would still miss Gustav, and I would love them and think about them every day, but I would not allow that love to be a source of pain anymore. This was a new day. This was Dakota. This was the spring.

The train pulled away and we looked around. I smiled nervously and greeted the other new colonists. I could tell on their faces, we were all feeling the same sense of awe and a little surprise. We could see everywhere in all directions, quite literally forever. There were hills and grass, as far as far as we could possibly see. On the horizon, a herd of what looked like very large cows was grazing. Buffalo, Father told me.

God and the Northern Pacific Railroad had given us this land, to homestead, to build our houses and families. We were going to grow crops and make a go of it, and we were going to do our best. Back in Germany, my father told stories about folks who did not have land like this to farm crops, and to raise families. They were crowded between two countries and peoples that are not their own. To become an American means to have personal freedom to have one's own hands in their own dirt, and be thankful to Almighty God for it.

The Dakota prairie is so big it can swallow you whole. The sky is so blue, it may well be an ocean above our heads. I know Heaven is there, and I look at that blue expanse and talk to my God. He comforts me. The grass goes on, forever. This opportunity is more Divine gift than governmental right. After the crowded neighborhood back home, with the sounds and smells of the city, I am a little daunted, I don't mind admitting, at the bigness of this space. But it is all ours. This is my adventure. This is why I was born. My mother and father risked everything in their journey from the Old World for me to come here, to build something new, where nothing has ever been. It is our Garden of Eden.

Of course we arrived to a vast emptiness. Sometimes it made me dizzy. There was no town, no lake, and no river. There was a man, John, who'd gone out ahead of the colony with the supply car, so he had a while to get used to the openness that the rest of us were just now experiencing. I wanted to know what he thought of it all. He had a way about him, a leadership, like my father has.

The men agreed the boxcars, in which we had arrived, would be the safest shelter for the time being. They had been detached from the train, and were on the sidetrack. There was enough sleeping room for all of us to have space, and before nightfall, campfires were burning outside the doorways of each car.

Bright and early the next morning, the men met to decide how to proceed. The railroad had sent lumber, in order that a building could be built — an immigrant house. While the children ran through the tall prairie grass and tried to capture prairie dogs, we women set about organizing our boxcars and supplies.

The men had the immigrant house built in a matter of days, and we all moved our blankets and kitchen wares, books and clothing. Our household goods went into that house, for we had left our old lives behind in Illinois, and brought little with us for a humble beginning. Anything minor was left in the boxcars. This was our new life, and we were building.

We were so thankful to have the immigrant house to stay in, after sleeping in the cold metal boxcars of a train!

It was not easy. But to go to the middle of nowhere and start something, you have to have to start from somewhere with a faith so strong, it bursts in your chest with every breath. We had no shelter, so we had to figure out what to live in, because winter would come the same time it did every year. Food was scarce.

After growing up in the crowded Chicago, it gave me great joy to garden with the other women. We grew beautiful food. It was so bright and colorful, the vegetables looked like flowers to me. Every color of the rainbow was represented in our garden, and things grew! They grew and grew as if they desired to reach the blue Heaven. Each day when the train passed through, a bag of bread was thrown from one of the cars, for one of the men had arranged with a baker in Bismarck to send food. We would hear the train coming, and run to be the first, and closest, to ensure we would catch something from that breadbag. It was not always enough. Every day, at least one of the townspeople went home emptyhanded. We were reminded of the miracle of the two fishes and five loaves of bread, and how it fed the multitudes. My mother never would have let anyone go hungry. That is why we started the garden. A garden does not depend on the 12:22 from the east. As the fruits and vegetables began to flourish and feed us that summer, we became bountifully thankful for them.

Soon, one of the more business-minded fellows ordered flour, rather than just bread, from Bismarck, and we all baked our own bread. That seemed to work better. For it is written, what you focus on, increases.

In thinking about what my mother would have done for this hungry, growing railroad town, I did what came naturally. I began cooking. One day, while my father was out working with the men, building what would become the main street of the settlement, I put as much food in the wagon as I could stuff onto the seat and took lunch to the men, as fast as I could.

Now, seeing as how there were only a few chickens in the yard, and I couldn't see my way clear to fry up my laying hens. We had laying chickens and we had eating chickens. I filled out this lunch with bread, zesty carrots, and cookies. They were not the easiest meals to eat while working, but I felt good about the food.

A garden, if it blooms, blooms with blessings straight from God, like manna from Heaven. Once we planted the garden, no one in the colony went without dinner again. We were so blessed, it was quite evident this is what we were supposed to be doing. We were meant to come out here, to Dakota Territory, and do God's work, and take care of each other, and build our homes, and he blessed us. The Sioux were much calmer and friendlier than we'd heard about, for at the turn of the century, when Lewis and Clark had travelled through this territory, they had informed these tribes they would now all be Americans.

Americans are what we all wanted to be. To be an American is why my father and my mother travelled by sea, and by train, to put everything they had into The United States and honor it every day, and they had my brother and me. We tried very hard to speak only English in our house, though we lived in a German neighborhood, and it was sometimes easy for my father to slip into Deutsch. Now, out here in Dakota, I felt even more American, if that was possible. Now, and here, we were building the nation.

One of the men had captured my curiosity. His name was John, like my father. He was amiable, and seemed very intelligent. He had a way of talking that made people listen to him, much like my father. I tried not to listen too closely, because that wouldn't be proper, but he always seemed very sure of himself, somewhat arrogant, but perhaps I imagined that, because he seemed to know everything. He appeared to be very interested in learning how to tame this vast, wild land. One day, those attentions turned to me, perhaps because we were about the same age. He and my father had been talking, as men do, and John came to me, and told me we were to be married.

We walked a while and talked, and I learned he had bravely come from Germany alone. His parents sent him away to America to avoid Catherine the Great's Reich, very much like when my mother had come to America many years ago, when she met my father. I found it ironic that basically a train brought John and me together, and a train had brought my mother and father together so long ago, travelling to a new land, to start a new life. It seemed Gustav was whispering to me, that this was the right thing to do. Gustav, my baby brother, must be somewhere on a train.

Before the wedding, a very special delivery came on the train. Father had sent for my mother's piano from our house in Chicago. He had helped a friend rebuild, whose music and ballet studio was nearly destroyed by The Great Fire. That this, this magnificent piano did not burn, was nothing short of miraculous. Mother's piano had been at the ballet studio ever since her fall, and during the time I was at school. I vowed to myself never to let harm come to this piano. Nothing would harm this, my prized possession, for I would play, "Edelweiss," and I could hear her sing. I could hear Mother tapping out the meter for me. We needed the music in New Salem. Hymns and music united us in our times of despair and joy. My piano would take care of the townspeople, all of them, the way she would have. She would have made them dance out of their misery. She would have sung them to sleep. My piano would always be here for them. I was overjoyed to be connected to my history with this piece of home. We had come here with so very little, and having Mother's piano here was very much like having her with me.

The year after the wedding, I gave birth to a daughter. She was small and smiley and perfect, and gleamed. I named her Elena. My cup runneth over.

Eggless, Milkless, Butterless Cake

2 c. sugar
2 c. water
2 T. shortening
1 c. raisins
1 tsp. each of soda, salt, cinnamon, nutmeg and cloves
3 c. flour

Boil for five minutes: sugar, water, shortening and raisins. When cool, add spices, soda and flour. Bake in loaves for one hour.

Zesty Carrots

1 pound carrots, peeled, cut in hunks, cook until tender
¼ c. water
2 T. grated onion
2 T. horseradish
½ c. Miracle Whip
½ tsp. salt
¼ tsp. pepper

Place cooked carrots in baking dish. Combine rest of ingredients and pour over carrots. Top with mixture of 1 T. butter, ¼ cup cracker crumbs and a dash of paprika. Bake at 375 for 30 minutes.

Kidnapping of Elena

HEATHER LINDSEY WAS A VERY NICE WOMAN.
People regarded her as mildly deranged, but she seemed
fine. She worked as hard as any of the men, in helping
to build the town and lifting and carrying lumber and
things she probably shouldn't be carrying.

Before coming to Dakota Territory, she, too, had
lived in Chicago. Heather Lindsey had lost her husband and children in the Great Fire. She had married
a second time, and, in hopes of building a family again,
had become pregnant twice. Both pregnancies ended
without a child in her arms. Heather Lindsey's second
husband was killed in the street in Chicago, after a
bad poker game. I often wondered, when I think of
her, how many times a heart can break before it just
stops beating?

One morning, we awoke early to find Elena miss-
ing. The front door was wide open. John's first instinct

was that our baby girl had been kidnapped by Indians, but when he ran out the door to hook up the wagon, he saw Mrs. Lindsey wandering away, sort of slowly and haphazardly, carrying my child. My husband walked straight up to her and ever-so gently took my baby back, without a word. Mrs. Lindsey kept walking away. The sun had not yet fully risen. We began locking our door after that night.

Lonely Winter

BECAUSE HE HAD THE DISTINCTION OF BEING THE
first pioneer of New Salem, of this whole area, John
felt responsible for the colony. He wanted us to have
a purebred herd of cows. He was passionate about the
subject. As the autumn wore on, John made the deci-
sion to spend the winter in Wisconsin, working in the
lumberyards, to earn the money for purebred Holsteins,
like the dairy cows back at his home in Germany. This
was for our future, he said. This sacrifice now would
benefit the future of our children, and their children.

I would miss him so terribly much. I asked him not
to go. We would till more acres and plant more wheat.
He felt very strongly that it was wise to do more work
now, so we would have more benefits later. When John
first broke ground in Dakota Territory, the old Sioux
had warned him, "Wrong Side Up," and my husband
honestly believed he shouldn't break any more ground

than was necessary. My father was here, he said, only as far away as the next homeplace. Our daughter and I would be fine.

When the eastbound train came through, my husband got on it, bound for the lumberyards of Wisconsin. It would be a cold, dangerous winter, for all of us.

The seasons were different on the prairie than they were in Chicago. I was trying to find new ways to keep the draft from coming in the door all the time. It seemed Old Man Winter wanted to share the holidays with my family.

Indeed, it was a cold winter. It was windy, which I have always known all about. I'm well-equipped to walk into the wind at a 45-degree angle to arrive at my destination, but when the snow was blowing sideways, and if it was too cold outside, I kept Elena inside our little house. Father would come over on nice days and help with securing the windows against the chill, or to play with my little girl. I appreciated having him nearby, and not away on a boat. If there had been a body of water anywhere close to us, Father would be sailing on it for weeks or a month at a time, and then both of the men in my life would have been gone all winter.

The homeplace was next to the railroad tracks. In those days, a lot of people rode the railroad, and when they would come to a settlement, and the train stopped, some people would detrain. Folks from the train or friendly Indians would come up to the house looking for food or a drink, and there I was, alone with a small child. I was scared out of my wits, but I had a gun. Father taught me to shoot that winter. I had heard a lady got shot in the chest at the hotel in town. It was apparently a misunderstanding, and there was no ill will involved, but I am quite certain that she can't be convinced of that. After all, she survived. I didn't want anyone, local or traveler, to shed blood in my house.

I longed for springtime and my husband's return. I looked forward to the day we would build a house. I wanted a nice, comfortable home for the rest of our lives. I knew that we couldn't live in the three-room homestead shack forever. I wanted to whitewash a house, and have glass windows, with lace curtains, and a big front porch. I wanted a big stone fireplace that would keep us warm on the blustery cold nights and days, and a kitchen. My kitchen would turn out the best kuchen in town. I would make fleischkeuchle and pies for church on Sundays. My kitchen would be bright, cheerful, and filled with wonderful smells, just like my mother's always had been.

Fleischkeuchle

6 c. flour
4 eggs
1 tsp. salt
1 c. milk
cream

Mix dry ingredients and milk. Add cream to form a soft dough. Set aside.

Ground meat
Minced onion and salt and pepper

Mix meat and spices. Shape into patties.

Using dough mixture, roll out into small circles. Place meat patties on bottom half of dough circle, fold the top half over the patty, and press with fingers around the patty to seal. Bake at 375 for 30-45 minutes.

Smoky

SMOKY HAD COME TO DAKOTA TERRITORY WITH
John. He kept the prairie beasts at bay. *Coyotes*, John
called them. They would howl, and Smoky would howl
louder. They would snarl, Smoky The Defender would
growl. We were his family, and he would not let those
coyotes get close to us at any price. On foggy morn-
ings, he would come up to the door, looking for his
food and some loving attention from me, and his fur
would be ever-so slightly damp from the moisture in
the air. We would feed him and pet him, but he never
stopped watching into the fog for predators. He always
was the protector. Smoky The Invincible. Smoky had
many adjectives. I named him something new every day.

Living in Chicago, I had not had a pet as a child,
so I did not know the companionship and love that
a dog would bring into my life. Smoky was our first
child. He knew my emotions — my joy and sadness and

worries, better than any of the other people in town did. One morning, I took the tin bowl of food for him outside. I never left his food outside, because I did not want vermin to get used to the idea that they could take up residence at my door. He was not waiting for me. I thought that was very strange.

I whistled. He did not come running. I called his name and got no response. There was no rustling in the grass, no stirring near the lean-to. This began to worry me, and I slowly stepped down the five steps, onto the prairie ground, calling Smoky's name again. And again, becoming slightly more frantic every time I said his name and he did not come bounding toward me through the prairie grass. Suddenly, I felt very alone in the world, and very afraid. I felt like a child. I remembered this fear — it was close to how I felt when my mother got hurt, and I knew in that instant, in that moment, seeing her lying on the parlor floor, bleeding from the side of her head, that nothing would be the same for us ever again. I wanted my brother there with me. I wished for Gustav. I felt so alone and lonely. Just then, far off in the foggy morning distance, I heard the familiar comfort of the train whistle. It sounded like my brother, grown now, telling me this would be alright. It sounded like a choir of angels breathing life into this distant, foreign land, whose spine was a railroad track.

And then, I found Smoky. He was about a hundred yards from the house, lying in the tall grass. He had obviously gotten into a quarrel with something overnight, probably a coyote. It looked like the coyote won. His fur was torn and the sight of him was so pitiful, I could not bear it. Smoky, who journeyed out to the frontier with this small group, had died protecting us. I sobbed as I walked back to the shack to get a shovel, but swallowed the lump in my throat before my little girl saw me and could get upset. I could not remember any time in my life, seeing my mother cry. I buried Smoky where he lay, so the coyotes would not bother him anymore. I fashioned a wooden marker, and wrote "SMOKY" on the cross.

Prairie Race

I AWOKE WITH A START, AND THE HOUSE FELT LIKE the train was coming through. No, I thought, the tracks are at least a hundred yards away. Why is it so loud tonight? Then, I heard a wail, and my sleepy ears could distinguish the pounding of hooves, which now rivaled the pounding in my chest. Daring barely to breathe, I tiptoed to the window in the front room, and peeked out at the night. The train was going through, yes, but on this side of the tracks were bison, dozens or hundreds of them. I wasn't sure which, for I couldn't count them while they ran in the dark across the snow-covered prairie. I glanced at Elena, sleeping in her bed, peacefully and mercifully unaware that at any moment, a rogue bison bull could cause their little prairie house to come crashing down, and bring their existence tonight to a standstill. I felt myself trembling, wanting to reach out and pick up her baby, but at the same time, not daring to wake her. The caboose was the last car, and as it waved goodbye from the tail of the train, the stampede slowed. My eyes had adjusted to the surreal light that shone down from the moon and reflected on the snow, illuminating the land and everything was clear now. The bison, those huge prairie animals, had been racing the train! I thought to myself, a wry smile on her lips, I wonder if they caught it. Just then, a knock at the door jolted me more than awake. I opened it to find Father standing there, and he scooped me up in his arms in a tight, protective embrace.

"I heard them," Father said in a low voice. "I would have come sooner."

Typically, the bison that we saw on the prairie were fairly docile and good-natured. They chewed on grass all day, roamed around the countryside, and now and again took a dirt bath, when they would roll back and forth on a hillside, looking very much like a dog with an itch to scratch. I wondered what had gotten into them that they decided to stampede tonight, and run with the train.

"Mountain lions," Father murmured. "I saw a pride up at Bluegrass, and they've been lying low, just waiting for their time to cause a peril."

John Returns in the Spring

WHEN THE CHINOOK WINDS BLEW, AND THE SNOW began to melt and get slushy, the train brought a vast rail car of lumber from Wisconsin and my husband back to me. That his return felt like springtime is an understatement. Elena jumped up into her papa's arms and screamed a shrill little girl scream of joy.

He had missed so much. We had done a lot of growing up while he was at the lumberyards. I guessed it had been the same for him. It had been a long, cold winter. One winter was a lot for a little girl. He looked around for Smoky. I shook my head, and glanced at the ground. He understood. John and Smoky were the first to spend a night alone on the prairie, and Smoky was the Royal Dog in this part of Dakota Territory. Now, I wondered where we would go from here, with one member of our family gone?

John took my hand and we walked toward the cars that had been unlatched when the train left. There was a platform car heaped with fresh lumber, to help get us started. The men would be building for a month. He disappeared inside the boxcar. I heard chickens. Chickens! He brought chickens! That meant we'd have eggs and there would be so much more!

Two pink snouts found their way into the spring air, as Jack and Emma emerged. Pigs! We have pigs? With a wider grin than I had ever seen on him, John proudly stepped down from the railcar's door, holding onto a lead. He took three steps forward, and Sue exited the car behind him. Sue! She was the cleanest young Holstein cow, with the most perfect black and white markings, and my husband was so proud, I couldn't help but feel unabashed glee in all of my being. Sue had a kind face, for a cow, and I knew there and then, that we would be good friends.

"You've been working hard," I said to him.

He nodded and held up Sue's lead, indicating that I should hold onto her. Being a girl from the city, I was nervous to hold onto a cow's rope, and not very certain what John was going to do next, but then he went back into the car, and brought out a young Holstein bull.

"This is Jefferson. President Jefferson bought this land, and now it is ours, and I will honor him by doing my very best with it and these cattle. Meet Jeff."

I thought to name the bull in honor of the president was appropriate. To continue the theme, the pigs were named Jabez and Jabez, for God was increasing our territory. The chickens did not get names. We felt they would not mind.

I had so much to tell John about our winter, and he had so much to tell me about his, that we almost didn't sleep for three days. All this time, these months, I had spent with Elena, teaching her to walk and talk, and telling her when the snow melted, her papa would come home to her. My winter with my little girl reminded me of all of my father's voyages when I was a girl, after we lost Gustav, and my mother and I were alone all that time. This time, Father was here to help me with my own child, and my husband had been gone for months, for the good of the homesteaders.

While out in the eastern part of the state, John had met important people, traveling for the Agricultural College in Fargo. For a time, it sounded like he wanted to move the family to the Fargo. I listened, and waited, to hear where his stories would inspire him to lead. Instead, because he was so proud to have his dream of his own land now, he worked to further the college's advancement throughout the state. He wanted to expand education throughout Dakota Territory, and ensure that all the homesteaders had the tools and wisdom to do the best they could with America's land.

He was so interested in education, and always wanted to learn more, to learn whatever he could about agriculture, for the old Sioux's words never left him: "Wrong side up." John had been overturning prairie grass to ready the fields for planting, and the Dakota men approached and warned him this land was better used for the grazing of cows, with its vast plains of grass that never end. These oceans of gold and green are nothing like the land near Chicago, where there is a different kind of sea. The lakes here are smaller than the big lake back in Illinois, but life-giving in their own way. John heeded the words, and our friendship with the Indians has been blessed.

John shared everything he learned with all of the farmers in the area. It was important to him that they all have the most information possible, in order that they use the best practices to care for the land. In this way, every farmer would be successful in raising his cattle and his crops, so his family would never be hungry.

My dream house was finished by May. When we moved in from our prairie shack, it may well have been a mansion. It had an upstairs, and a full kitchen, a front porch, and glass windows! The boards were white-washed, just like in my dreams, and I had windowboxes for my flowers. Elena's room was at the back of the house, and my bedroom had large windows, overlooking much of the farm. There was another bedroom, to be made ready for the son we were hoping to receive later in the year. I could see so much of the town from my house! John had a library on the first floor. We had a back door now, and a picket fence. Now, my garden would not be as easily plundered by various creatures of the prairie. My clothesline was behind the house, and the barn was beyond. Jeff, Sue and Kupfer the horse would come hang their heads over the fence, looking for an apple or a little attention. Sometimes, they reminded me of Smoky.

I remember the night clearly. I was cleaning up after our evening meal, and I heard a howl. Alarmed, I gestured to Elena to go into the other room. John was in his library reading farming manuals from the agricultural college, and I believe he did not hear the first howl. Thinking a coyote had brazenly made its way to our front door, I approached with my shotgun. I caught myself creeping on tiptoe. When I opened the door a few inches, the most beautiful she-wolf looked back at me with ice blue eyes. She lay down and whimpered at the sight of my gun. At first, I wasn't sure what to think, but that this wolf was half-tame. Then, something tugged at my heart and told me to feed her, because she may be carrying babies. After all, our baby was due soon, and I didn't want this she-wolf's babies to go without. My next thought was that I did not want a coyote sticking around my house, so I shouldn't give her something to eat. Compassion won that battle, and she got some of the bones from our supper. I closed and latched the door, and didn't think of her again, until the morning, when I came down the stairs and opened my beautiful front door to greet the sunshine, and John called out in surprise. There she was, sitting like Queen of Sheba, triangular ears pert atop her furry head, waiting for me.

I was hanging wet laundry on my clothesline that afternoon while John was stacking some rocks. Mr. Luck, a businessman in town, drove his team of horses up and tied them in front of the house.

"Good afternoon, John. Mrs. Christiansen," he said, nodding toward me. The wolf dog was at full attention as soon as Mr. Luck had driven up in his wagon, but did not make a sound, which I thought was odd.

"A Siberian Husky!" Mr. Luck exclaimed, as he directed his attention to the wolf dog that had made itself very at home on our porch. "I haven't seen one of you since the old country!"

While rubbing her ears and making very good friends, he went on to explain that we had a female

Siberian Husky, and it looked like she was full grown. The three of us stood for a while, musing about how she could have gotten here, and why she seemed to have adopted us, The Christiansens, but we were very glad she did. She was friendly and beautiful. She seemed harmless, and not nearly forboding enough, so we may need another dog, in time, around the farm. This would be a good companion for me and the children. She needed a name. I had decided she had a Queen of Sheba look to her.

"Sheba," I looked in her direction, and she came to me. "Sheba. Is that your name?"

Sheba sat down, ears at attention, waiting for my next instructions. I loved her intensely, now that I knew I could keep her as part of the family. Sheba became my instant companion, and best friend. We were blessed with a son, just as we'd hoped, on an autumn morning, in the middle of harvest. John named him Theodore. I cried tears of happiness, for now Elena would never be alone.

The Church Roof

MY HUSBAND AND MR. LUCK SADDLED UP THE riding horses and headed out across the pasture to inspect the fence line. They were discussing plans for tree lines and field rotation, and I really didn't understand any of that, or want to bother with it.

The church was being built. I asked Father to take me and Elena into town to see the progress on the church building. I wanted to help any way we could. I had picked several tomatoes from the garden that morning, so I quickly put together some tomato sandwiches, and we were on our way. When we arrived in town, my breath was taken away. I was so proud of my fellow homesteaders. Everyone was pitching in, all those people had a role. I greeted them and we were welcomed by Mrs. Doberchinska. I offered the tomato sandwiches I'd made for the people building the church, and she thanked me and took them and placed them on a rough-hewn table with other food for those working.

Father had joined the men working, and was already halfway up a ladder, on his way to the roof. I gathered Elena, and shared with her one of the tomato sandwiches I'd made. I had found some lemonade in the kitchen, and as soon as she had two bites, she ran off to play with the other children. I wandered around the church-to-be area, visiting with the different groups of people gathered there. Families were picnicking, people were taking a break from working and were eating their lunch, and it looked like we had come to visit at just the right time.

I glanced up at the roof of our church building, and said a prayer, thanking God for this opportunity, this land, and this beautiful place. I thanked Him for my family, our blessings, and for everything that had brought us here.

I heard the train coming. It was a ways off, but it would be coming through soon. My Father heard the whistle, too. His chin jutted toward Heaven momentarily as he looked up and to the east. Though he knew the train would be coming, as we all had become accustomed to the daily run by now, this jerking motion of his chin surprised the rest of his body, and he lost his balance. I would have screamed, if I'd had the time.

Father slid down the side of the roof, unable to stop himself by grasping for the new eaves of the church, scraping up his arms beneath his shirt as he slid. He fell to the ground in front of me as heavily and gently as a stone's throw.

My mind raced in that moment. I could not fathom that this was happening again, just like Mother.

But this fall was not like Mother's. She had hit her head on the steely, icy rock of Lake Michigan. This soft, blessed Dakota earth had caught Father, and I knew that it would be alright. I had to believe, and when he heard the train come close and opened his eyes, I knew I was right. This was a place that could heal.

"Gustav?" Father asked, weakly. He searched my eyes for an answer. It nearly broke my heart. I wanted Gustav to be here as well. I thought of my little brother every time I heard that train, but no, Papa. Gustav — he is not here now.

Some of the men had stopped working on the building, and lifted Father into the wagon, that I could take him home. The church women helped me round up Elena, and gave her kuchen. She was calm and quiet, and held her baby brother, who was oblivious to my anxiety. What a good girl, I thought, as I was silently thankful that by behaving so well, she was such a help to me during this terrifying moment.

I drove the horses back to our homeplace, and John was out in front, finishing the pickets on the gate in front of the house. When he saw that I was driving, and Father was slumped over in the seat, he knew right away something was drastically wrong. He put his hammer down, stood up, and watched as we approached. When I awkwardly halted the team, John took hold of and tied up the horses before I could jump down from the wagon. While I ushered my little girl into the house, John carried my father in over his shoulder and put him in the downstairs parlor, on the hassock. He had come to.

Father was awake. He was able to talk. He told us there was tremendous pain in his side, and it was difficult for him to be on his feet. He could not walk, but his mental function was intact. That was a blessing. I was so glad to have my father still with me.

We had some long discussions about what to do with Father's farm. It was decided my husband would take it over. Our homestead was twice as large as most, being that I had travelled to Dakota Territory as a single woman and my Father would move into our house, so I could take care of him, and John planned to use some of my claim for pasture, and his own for wheat. We would farm Father's fields as well as ours. With the addition of the livestock, the added land would be useful. This was a big change, and required a lot of work, but my father needed our help. It is customary in the old country, for the young to care for the old. My husband fashioned a walking stick for him out of an elm branch, and Father was able to get from one room to another, with pain. He never ascended the stairs again.

Father would help me with the garden, and he had knowledge from the old country to make vegetable plants more productive that he had never shared before, perhaps because he spent most of my childhood on a ship. These were planting secrets from his mother, my grandmother, he told me. I just needed him to stay in one place long enough, to till a row for peas. He chuckled.

We wanted to do more for the men building all of the buildings in town, especially since our house was finished and we felt safe and warm and were grateful for this, with the winter coming. It seemed here, in the Northland, winter was always coming. We were always working, preparing for the onslaught of the wind and cold of winter. Father would keep me company while I cooked and baked and filled the wagon with as much food as I could, then I would take it to town to feed the builders. May we all be safe and warm when the wind blows.

One summery day, we decided to take Father over to his homeplace, a quarter-mile away. He wanted to visit his house and farm. He had not been there since the fall. This was no small undertaking. I put two pillows and a quilt into a cart that John readied in the front of the house, and helped Father into it, with his walking stick, so he could get around his little house once we gungled across the field.

We took him on quite a bumpy ride over to his homeplace in a small cart with only one horse leading us. The ride through the tall prairie grass was nothing short of an adventure! After we had traveled halfway, we realized there was no going back, and we might as well trudge on. I know, given my father's history on the high seas, that even though this was hard, he was enjoying it, because he would laugh between wincing in pain.

It was cathartic in a way, to see his prairie house and gather some things. There were a still a few photographs of my mother in that house that I wished to have in my own home, and Father wanted his pen to write a journal. John and I did not see any harm in leaving the house open and as it was, with the bed and simple washstand, in the event of travelers seeking refuge from prairie wind. We took a moment to remember what it had been like when we first came to Dakota Territory, and we agreed that since Father's home was with us, we did not need to be risking his life like that again. The bumpy ride across the field was emotional for all of us, and tiring.

Father grew weaker and paler everyday. I thought he enjoyed being around his grandchildren. They were good for his mood, although he tired easily. He was no longer able to milk Sue, or feed the chickens. One day, he began coughing. It was moderate coughing, but coughing just the same. He stayed in bed all the time now, and was no longer able to muster the strength to get out on the porch and watch the birds and dogs. I brought him all of his meals and coffee in his room.

Soon, he fell asleep. He did not wake up. My father's breathing slowed, and eventually, on a fall day, my adventurous Father passed from this earth into Heaven. I miss him every single day. He was a hero to every person who knew him.

Elena cried. Oh, she cried and she cried. That is what was the hardest for me, hearing her raw emotion, and explaining to her that Opa had gone away. Teddy was too young to understand this. This was too early for both of them, really.

Elena, I hope you have a daughter. I hope she is every bit as funny and full of personality as you are. I love our tea parties and playing with you.

Teddy, my strong little man. You will no doubt inherit your father's love for this Dakota Territory. Anything he can learn and teach about the land, he will. Do well.

My dear children, remember that family is the most important thing there is. You cannot take your whitewashed house with glass windows or your riches to Heaven with you. But you can take your children and your family.

NORTH DAKOTA, 2013

SOPHIA PASSED FROM THIS WORLD TO THE NEXT during the birth of her third child in 1905. The child did not survive. Commemorating her is the largest statue and headstone in the cemetery, and John lived alone with the children, heartbroken, for years before taking another wife. Her well-built whitewashed house with glass windows still stands, and tourists wander through it, musing life in the pioneering days of Dakota Territory.

No longer is it the Big Eighties. I don't wear big lavender bows in my hair as often anymore and I haven't practiced on that piano in more than twenty-five years. My parents sold the house. They moved into one of those swanky condominiums that people buy when they retire. You know the type — the curtains are already selected to match the designer walls and carpets, so Mom had to go buy new retirement furniture and dishes. Sophia's piano found a new home — on loan — with one of the museums in the local histori-cal society. This means that it still belongs to me. This arrangement gives the piano the opportunity to be enjoyed by museum visitors, who may marvel over the fact that this wooden behemoth survived The Great Chicago Fire, the expansion into Dakota Territory, and the pounding of children's hands. It was on a trip home for a class reunion that I ventured to the museum, the site of my first paying job, to visit my piano.

From the Lawrence Welk display I saw her. Pretty creative, I thought, to hook up a bubble machine in the champagne music corner. That little girl couldn't have been more than four, and her parents, aunt and uncle were enthralled with the kitchen and bathroom setup in the back of the museum. She, herself, was chasing bubbles, as children will do.

"Yeah, this is some good old German workman-ship here," Brandon muttered from beneath the table. "There are two leaves. Hey, honey, we should see if they'll sell this."

Jackie, Mrs. Brandon, smiled with a little boredom. She was glowing at the prospect of new furniture, but she was also well aware she was in a museum, not a furniture store.

"You should be able to build that, huh, Bran?" rec-ommended Shannon, Brandon's younger brother, and the one of the two with more attitude. The brotherly love and sibling rivalry never ends with these two, I thought, reflecting on high school football.

The little blonde Shirley Temple was off to her own exploring. While chasing Lawrence Welk's "champagne music" bubbles, her fingers found the red velvet rope surrounding the piano, in the nearby Music through History display. A velvet rope is lovely, but it is no security against four-year-old girls. As curiously as a kitten, she climbed up onto the seat of my great-great grandmother's one hundred, fifty-year-old piano, and ran her fingers along the decorative cutouts in the wood. There was no varnish on this wood. It was not shiny. It was honest teak, crafted sometime around the Civil War by someone who loved music and respected the wood. The piano tuner who came to the house when I was a kid used to say he could hear "voices in this old piano."

That registered with me. The piano spoke to me too. It told me to go places. Take the train. See the big city, and probably Europe if I can. Learn to cook. Sing joyfully. Love wholeheartedly. Laugh out loud. Don't cry.

I glanced up from the curly blonde head as she timidly touched Middle C. Over at her little family gathering in the kitchen display, still no one noticed she'd wandered off. That's okay. I'll hang out with her at the piano. It'll be much more fun than discussing the engineering of tables and chairs. The book of music on the piano's music stand was open to "Edelweiss."

Yes, I thought. Bless my homeland forever.

Coming Soon from Author Josie Blaine...

NOWHERE AND EVERYWHERE: A Good Place To Be From

GERTIE

It was one of those sunny spring days at the cusp of summer in Durham, North Dakota, when not one of the thirty-one high school seniors could concentrate on Mr. Anderson's U. S. History lecture. Gertrude was listening. She really was, with her droopy eyes occasionally glancing at Mr. Anderson. The warmth of the April afternoon rays through the window was hitting her desktop and making it hard for her to focus any longer on the influx of the immigrants in the Nineteenth Century. What had the lion's share of her attention was out the window.

Two of last year's senior boys, Spencer and Billy Ray, were building on Old Man Christianson's house across the street from school. Spencer planned on marrying Mary Schultz this summer, and that would be their house. Spencer and Mary had been going out together all through high school, so it was a given they would have a June wedding. Mary was going to be a teacher, just like she'd planned to be since she'd set up a teddy bear and porcelain doll classroom in her room in third grade. She would be off Mayville this fall at the Teacher's College. Spencer would miss her, but he would be working hard at the lumber mill, and saving up as much money as he could, and fixing up that house. Mary would be home on Christmas breaks, and her schooling would be finished in a year. Until then, Spencer would be baching it, but it would not be all that difficult for him, as his mother and sisters would still be cooking for him. Mary was the one who had to go away from her world, and be truly independent, Gertrude thought.

Gertrude wondered about college. Some girls went to the Teacher's College, then worked as teachers and got married and stopped working for good or for a while. She really thought it sounded fun when she heard the stories from some of her older friends, returning for the summer break. Her friends who had gone on to the Teachers' school spent a lot of time getting to know other girls, and learning about more than just math and history. There was a boys' school in a nearby town, and wouldn't you just know it, those boys would come around, looking for dates to the social events. Dances were held at either college on holidays, and Gertrude heard of some of the girls dressing as flappers. That sounded like a whole lot of fun. She wanted to dress up.

She wanted to be colorful and she wanted to be pretty and have everyone look at her and maybe even have a few boys flirt with her. Gertrude looked down at her farm girl shoes and absentmindedly reached up and twirled a henna golden red curl on her shoulder, and figured those kind of fantasies were not for dairy barn girls. She might as well accept it; this was her lot in life. This was where she would be forever. She looked down at the start of a blister on her otherwise tender right hand and she knew there would be more as the summer wore on. Her skin would get brown as an Indian's. Her hands would get a little rougher, carrying the cream cans to town every week, to sell at the creamery for grocery money, and her farm girl shoes, they would scuff up. After they saw how harvest went this fall, she would get some new clothes. That is just how it went every year on the farm.

Kyle and Zack did the lion's share of the farm work, but there was no shortage of work to be done on a farm. From sun up to sun down, someone had to gather eggs, feed chickens, and bale the hay. Never was there a moment they were not baling hay, it seemed. Those horses and cows always needed to eat. If the cows did not eat, there would be nothing to sell at the creamery, and then there would be no shoes, no haircuts, no new coats.

Gertrude did try sewing a couple of winters ago. She made Zack a shirt to go to a school dance with Peggy Warren. That purple shirt was such a disaster, and persnickety old Peggy Warren was so embarrassed, she never spoke to Zack again. He told his little sister to mind her own business and they would get their shirts in town, thank you very much. Gertrude thought that may not have had so much to do with her sewing skills, as it did a particular disastrous sloppy French kissing incident that the whole town knew about and Zack just wouldn't admit.

Gertrude knew there had to be more; there had to be more than just Durham, North Dakota. She would like to see what else was out there, but she wasn't so sure she wanted to go to the Teacher's school, in order to spend the rest of her life working in a school.

When Mr. Anderson dismissed class, Gertrude gathered her books, lined them up carefully in her knapsack, in A-B-C order, because that is how she liked things, and slung it over her shoulder. She lifted her lunch pail with her left hand, from the floor where it had been all day, its cheese sandwich and apple still tidily placed inside. She hadn't had much of an appetite lately, and she didn't seem to be hungry, either. Maybe she was depressed, or nervous about her future after graduation. Or she was in love.

Go to www.JosieBlaine.com to pre-order your own copy of "Nowhere and Everywhere"

CPSIA information can be obtained at www.ICGtesting.com
Printed in the USA
LVOW08s2337040414

380461LV00001B/217/P